Walter's Wand

Walter's Wand

Story by Eric Houghton
Illustrations by Denise Teasdale

softbABCks

Text copyright © 1989 Eric Houghton
Illustrations copyright © 1989 Denise Teasdale

First published in Great Britain in 1989 by **ABC**

This edition first published in 1992 by softbacks,
an imprint of **ABC**, All Books for Children,
a division of The All Children's Company Ltd
33 Museum Street, London WC1A 1LD

Printed and bound in Hong Kong

British Library Cataloguing in Publication Data
Houghton, Eric
Walter's wand.
I. Title   II. Teasdale, Denise

823.914 [J]

ISBN 1-85704-015-5

To Cecile — who made it all possible

Walter made a magic wand.
He found a fairly straight stick and covered it with scraps of coloured silver paper. He practised waving it about.

"Does it work?" asked his Mum.
"When I use magic words," he told her.

Walter took his wand to the library.
"Please don't poke," said the librarian,
when the wand pushed over
some leaflets.

"Please don't meddle," said the
librarian, when Walter played
with the index cards.

"Please don't touch," said the librarian, when he built a castle with the dictionaries. Walter looked at her.

"Walter," said his Mum quickly, "find a book to read—and keep out of mischief."

Behind a bookcase, Walter gave his wand a quick practice-wave.

"Ploppa-gooksniff," he said, saying the first magic word that came into his head. Then he tapped the nearest book with his wand; it was called "Tigers".

Trees sprouted from the floor. Vines and orchids twisted round the shelves. Apes swung from the lights and snakes slithered among the magazines.

Walter felt hot and sticky.

Then seven tigers came prowling from behind
the bookcases, snarling and looking hungry.
Walter was delighted.

But the librarian didn't get eaten.
She put everyone on top of a
bookcase and sprinkled drawing-pins on
the floor around it. The tigers tried to reach
her, but the pins made them hop and howl.
"And please don't scratch the furniture,"
the librarian told them.

Walter was disappointed; he thought the tigers should have been braver. He reached down with his wand and tapped the "Tigers" book.

At once the jungle disappeared and
everything was back to normal.
"Haven't you found a book yet,
Walter?" asked his Mum.

Walter saw the librarian was watching him.
He went behind another bookcase.

"Oogla-pluntium," he said, then tapped another
book with his wand. It was called "Pirates".

Palm trees and rocks grew out of the pale, sandy
floor. Parrots flew round the shelves and lizards
scuttled over the encyclopaedias.

Walter felt dry and dusty.

Eleven pirates leapt out, desperate for someone to kidnap. Walter was pleased they looked so fierce.

But the librarian wasn't dragged off in chains.
Piling up dictionaries, she built a fortress
on her counter and brought everyone
inside. And when the pirates began
waving their cutlasses and uttering
blood-curdling threats, she drove them
off by shooting pencils at them with
an elastic band.
"And don't damage the books with
those cutlasses," she told them.

Walter was disappointed; he thought the pirates could have tried harder. He touched the "Pirates" book with his wand. At once the pirates disappeared and everything was back to normal.

"Don't stand about dreaming, Walter,"
said his Mum. "Find a book!"

The librarian was still frowning at Walter,
so he stepped behind another bookcase.
"Quoggley-squint-box," he said and
tapped another book with his wand.
It was called "Oceans".
Green waves surged through the library.
Seaweed climbed over the counters.
Lobsters crawled among the books.
Dolphins splashed and played.
Walter felt cold and wet.

But the librarian wasn't swept away. She quickly built
a boat by stapling together three bookcases, labelled
"A", "R" and "K". Then she put everyone on board
and made them paddle round the library.
"And please stop balancing those
books on your noses," she
told the dolphins.

Walter forgot to be disappointed; he was too busy enjoying himself. He could make bigger splashes than anyone else.

At last he leaned out of the boat and tapped the "Oceans" book with his wand. The water subsided and everything was back to normal.

"You want all those, Walter?" asked his Mum. "And I thought you were just day-dreaming . . ."

Walter looked down. He had one book about tigers, one about pirates and one about oceans.

He took them to the counter and the librarian dated them. Then he dropped his wand into the wastebin: he realised the magic must never have happened.

"That wand is far too good to throw away!" said the librarian, and she put it back into his hand.

Walter stared at her.

Then he saw the bit of palm-leaf in her hair — and the seaweed under her collar — and her sudden, warm smile.